Dear Reader,

There are many different ways to earn a trophy. Whether it's from playing sports, working hard at school, or lending a helping hand in your community, receiving a trophy can be a very exciting moment. It represents hard work, dedication, and effort you put in to whatever you are trying to accomplish.

My favorite award that I've won is my World Series trophy. I dreamed of winning the World Series as a kid. It's the pinnacle of playing baseball, and it takes a total team effort. It makes everything you have worked so hard for worth it—all the years of practice and training, minor league games, and major league seasons. My teammates and I will cherish that win for the rest of our lives. The coolest part is that we did it together.

I hope that each and every one of you gets a chance to experience earning a "World Series" trophy. Continue to be honest, be kind, be responsible, show effort, and work as hard as you can for yourself and the people around you. Have fun along the way and a trophy can soon be in your hands to enjoy and appreciate.

LITTLE

Rhino

LITTLE

Rhino

by RYAN HOWARD and KRYSTLE HOWARD

⚾ **BOOK SIX** ⚾

TROPHY NIGHT

SCHOLASTIC INC.

To Matt, Rich, and our team who helped make this series possible.

Thank you.

—R.H. & K.H.

· CHAPTER 1 ·
The Trophy Shelf

Rhino ran his fingers over the letters on the trophy: MVP.

Most Valuable Player. The shiny metal baseball player was frozen in mid-swing at the top of the trophy. *He's smacking a home run,* Rhino thought.

Rhino had hit quite a few homers for the Mustangs. He'd been having a great baseball season. But the trophy wasn't his. It belonged to his brother, C.J., from two years ago.

Rhino's first baseball season was nearing its end. He hoped he'd soon be bringing home a trophy like C.J.'s.

MVP of this league. Then record-setting home-run hitter in middle school. Player of the Year in high school and college. Then the Major Leagues. The All-Star Game! The World Series! World Series champions!

Rhino admired the trophy again, feeling the smooth metal.

"Making room for my new one?" C.J. said with a laugh as he entered the living room. Rhino and his older brother looked a lot alike, but C.J. was taller and more muscular. They both had a quick smile.

"Or mine," Rhino said. He set the trophy back on the ledge, between C.J.'s championship basketball and soccer trophies.

Grandpa James had set up a shelf in the living room and filled it with all of their awards. Rhino spent a lot of time looking at the various trophies and plaques they had collected as a family.

"Here's the most important one yet," said Grandpa James, following C.J. into the room. He held C.J.'s latest award—a third-place plaque from the middle-school science fair. Sports were very important in Grandpa James's house, but school and learning always came first. C.J.'s prizewinning poster about Jupiter's moons had taken a lot of brainwork. He'd stayed up late several nights researching the facts, and then he carefully drew the moons circling the giant planet.

"That's quite a lineup of awards," Grandpa said, placing his hand on Rhino's shoulder. "And there will be one for you soon. Every player in your baseball league gets a trophy for taking part."

Rhino nodded, but just "taking part" wasn't enough for him. He wanted a trophy for best hitter, or all-star first baseman, or most home runs. And another one for winning the championship. The Mustangs had hit a rough stretch and lost their two most recent games, but they could wrap up a spot in the playoffs by winning their final regular-season game this weekend. From there, they'd have a shot at the title.

C.J. pointed to an older trophy behind the

others. "There's Grandpa's league championship award from high school basketball," he said. "That's a big-time trophy."

"We won that game on a last-second shot," Grandpa said. "I grabbed a rebound, gave a quick fake, then dished the ball to my teammate. He scored at the buzzer."

Everybody in this family has won major sports awards, Rhino thought. *Except me.* His only contribution to the table was a blue ribbon from the school talent show. He'd performed with two of his teammates and won first prize, but most of that credit belonged to Carlos, the singer in the Mustang Rock band. Rhino had helped Carlos gain enough confidence to use his great singing voice in the talent show.

Rhino's thinker told him not to worry. He'd earn a sports trophy soon.

"Little Rhino, you should hear more about how C.J. earned that MVP trophy," Grandpa said.

"For being the star of your team, right?" Rhino asked.

Grandpa shrugged. "He was a star, but . . . were you the best hitter on that team, C.J.?"

C.J. shook his head. "Bobby had a higher batting average."

"And you didn't hit the most home runs, did you?"

C.J. laughed. "I didn't hit *any* home runs that season. I wasn't as strong then as Rhino is now."

Rhino found that hard to believe. C.J. was so strong. He'd hit a lot of homers this year for his middle-school team.

"Seems to me you weren't the star pitcher either," Grandpa said. "But you did many things well, C.J. The best thing you did was support your teammates. You were the team leader. You always had a positive voice with everybody, whether they hit a home run or struck out."

I do that, too, Rhino thought. *Maybe I am an MVP.*

"Of course, he was an excellent player, too," Grandpa said. "But there a lot of things that go into being an MVP."

They celebrated C.J.'s science award with Grandpa's spaghetti and meatballs, then ice cream for dessert. Rhino scooped out the chocolate chip ice cream and drizzled it with chocolate syrup. He added a fresh strawberry to the top of the pile. *It looks a little like a trophy,* Rhino thought. He imagined his coach handing him a huge baseball trophy—just like C.J.'s but a foot taller. The lettering said PLAYER OF THE YEAR.

"What are you waiting for?" C.J. asked. "Your dessert will melt."

Rhino nodded. He took a big spoonful and grinned. "I was just thinking," he said. "Hopefully soon we'll have a celebration dinner for me."

· CHAPTER 2 ·
Bases Loaded

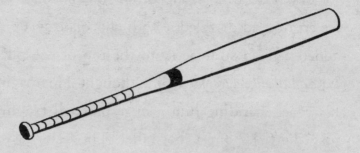

Rhino smacked his hand into his glove and eyed the runner at first base. "Let's turn two!" he called to the infielders. A *turn two* would be a double play that ends the inning and maintains the Mustangs' one-run lead.

It had been a wild game, with the Wolves taking a 2–0 lead back in the first inning before there were any outs. But Dylan had settled down for the Mustangs and struck out three batters in a row. Then the Mustangs stormed back with four runs in the bottom of the first inning, including an RBI double by Rhino.

The lead seesawed back and forth for several innings. In the top of the fifth, Rhino led off with a walk, stole two bases, and scored from third on a wild pitch. That gave the Mustangs a 7–6 lead.

"Come on, Dylan!" called Rhino's teammates. "Strike this guy out!"

The batter sent a bouncing rocket up the middle, skimming past Dylan's glove. Cooper darted over from shortstop and snagged the ball. He flipped it to Carlos at second base for an out.

Rhino's eyes widened as Carlos's throw to first soared too high. With the batter storming toward the base, Rhino leaped, knocking the ball down with the tip of his glove. The ball skipped into right field, but Rhino ran after it, and the runner did not try for second.

"Two outs," Rhino called as he flipped the ball to Dylan. He held up two fingers and waved to his teammates.

The day was hot. Rhino wiped his sweaty forehead with the back of his hand and pulled his cap into place. He wanted a drink of water. "Let's end this inning!" he yelled.

Falling behind this late in the game would mean trouble. If the Mustangs lost, their season would be over.

I like baseball too much to let that happen, Rhino thought. *I wish we could play all summer!*

Rhino had studied the league standings before the game. With a win, the Mustangs' final record would be eight wins and four losses. That would put them in a tie for second place. But a loss today would drop their record to 7-5—in a tie for fourth with the Wolves. Since only four teams would make the playoffs, the final spot would go to the Wolves based on today's result.

The runner at first base took a big lead. Rhino knew that the kid was fast. He could score from first on a double.

Dylan wound up and threw a fastball.

Whack! The ball sped toward right field. Rhino dove, leaving his feet and stretching as far as he

could go. He grabbed the line drive, rolling in the grass and squeezing the ball tight. He held up his glove.

"Out!" called the umpire.

Rhino smiled. His teammates cheered as they ran to the dugout.

"Super catch!" said Bella, running in from right field. She grabbed Rhino's hand and helped him to his feet. "That ball would have reached the fence. He hit it so hard it might have smashed through it!"

The Mustangs had the top of their batting order coming up: Cooper, Bella, and Dylan. Rhino would bat fourth—the cleanup hitter—as long as someone got on base.

"Big inning!" Rhino said. "Let's wrap this up." He was puffing from excitement. Making that catch had been a thrill.

Rhino took a long swig of water. "How's your arm?" he asked Dylan. "You've thrown a lot of pitches today."

"I'm fine," Dylan replied, staring out at the

field. Dylan was never very friendly, but he and Rhino had grown to respect each other as teammates. "The hot weather keeps me loose."

Cooper popped the ball into left field behind the shortstop. It looked like an easy out. But the shortstop and the left fielder both ran toward it, then stopped when they saw each other, thinking the other player was going to catch it. The ball fell softly to the grass between them, and Cooper reached first base with a single.

Bella made a perfect bunt down the third-base line, moving Cooper to second. Better yet, she beat the catcher's throw to first.

"Way to hustle, Bella!" Rhino called.

Two on, no outs.

"Bring them home, Dylan," Rhino said, stepping into the on-deck circle. He took a few easy swings. *Cause if you don't, I will,* Rhino's thinker said.

The Wolves' coach called time-out and walked to the mound. He spoke to the pitcher for a minute, then waved to the third baseman. "Pitching change," the coach called to the umpire. The third baseman and the pitcher switched positions.

Dylan walked over to Rhino as the new pitcher warmed up. "This guy's in my gym class at school, so I've seen him pitch." Dylan whispered. "He's even wilder than that first pitcher. If he can't find the strike zone, I'll get a walk."

Rhino nodded. Dylan's guess was right. The pitcher managed just one strike.

"Ball four!" the umpire called. "Take your base."

Dylan trotted to first, and Cooper and Bella moved up. The bases were loaded.

The rest of the Mustangs rattled the dugout fence as Rhino stepped up. Rhino was a power hitter—he'd hit more home runs than anyone in the league.

"A walk's as good as a hit," Carlos called from outside the dugout. He'd be up next.

Be patient, Rhino told himself. *Carlos is right.* Cooper would score if Rhino drew a walk.

But we'll all score if I hit it out of the park, he thought.

"Strike one!" was the call as the first pitch zipped past.

"That's it, Larry!" yelled the catcher. He threw the ball back. "He just needed to find his groove," the catcher said, mostly to himself.

Rhino glanced down at the catcher, then gripped the bat tighter.

The second pitch was high and outside. Rhino watched it go past.

"Good eye!" Carlos called. "Wait for your pitch."

Rhino took a quick look at the three base runners. All were taking short leads off the bases, leaning forward and ready to run. Rhino dug his toe into the dirt.

The next pitch looked perfect—waist-high and fast. *BAM!* Rhino's swing was hard but smooth. Nothing ever felt better than the bat meeting the ball and sending it soaring. Rhino knew it was gone the second he hit it. *Bye-bye baseball,* he thought. He dropped the bat and sprinted toward first base, watching the ball fly deep over the center fielder's head.

A grand slam home run!

Rhino felt like he was dreaming as he ran around the bases. Cooper, Bella, and Dylan waited at home plate, patting his back and yelling as he scored.

He slapped hands with Carlos as he walked by. "Way to go," Carlos said. "You just put this game out of reach."

I sure hope so, Rhino thought. The Wolves would bat one more time. In a wild game like this one, anything could happen.

Carlos hit a single, but that was the end of the rally. The Mustangs took the field with an 11–6 lead.

Dylan seemed as strong as ever. Just as in the first inning, he struck out three batters in a row. Game over.

The Mustangs were in the playoffs!

· CHAPTER 3 ·
Bella's Big Secret

What a great season," Coach Ray said as the players gathered in the dugout after the game. "I couldn't be prouder of this team. You've been good sports whether we win or lose, and you've worked hard at your baseball skills. So I'm very glad that we'll be playing an extra game or two in the playoffs."

Dylan raised his hand. "Do we get trophies if we win the championship?"

"Yes," Coach said. "But let's not be too concerned about that. First of all, the playoffs are a chance to have more fun."

"But we want to win!" Bella said. "Right, Dad?"

Coach Ray laughed and patted his daughter's head. "And since you're wondering about trophies, there will be a few special team awards at the end of the season. Best Pitcher, Best Hitter, Best Fielder, and Most Improved Player."

Why not Most Valuable Player? Rhino thought. Dylan was probably the best pitcher on the team. He and Cooper usually alternated as pitcher and shortstop. Rhino didn't pitch, so he wouldn't win that award.

Best Hitter? Rhino was the most *powerful* hitter, but Cooper and Dylan both had higher batting averages. Not by much, though. So Rhino had a chance to win that one. Rhino hoped Dylan wouldn't win two awards. Dylan was a great player and he'd become a better teammate, but he was a big-mouthed bully to the other players early in the season—he was even a bully to Rhino.

Too bad there isn't a sportsmanship award, Rhino thought. He would probably win that. He always played fair and supported his teammates. And he

was the first one in line to congratulate the other team after a game, no matter which team won.

Was Rhino the Mustangs' best fielder? He'd made a few errors this season, but so had everybody else. First base was a tough position. He had to handle lots of batted balls, and throws from all over the field. So he *might* be the best fielder, but it was hard to say.

All of the Mustangs had improved a lot over the season. Rhino had become a better hitter and a better first baseman. But he'd been pretty good right from the start. Some of the other players improved a lot more, even if they weren't as good as Rhino yet.

Don't worry about the awards, his thinker told him. *Just keep playing hard and have fun. There's nothing more that I can do.*

Still, a special award would be great. Especially after such a successful season. Rhino was a little disappointed that none of the awards sounded like a perfect match for him. But then he remembered

Grandpa's "three second" rule. He could be sad or angry about something for three seconds, but then it was time to look on the bright side. Like that major grand slam he'd just hit!

"Our first playoff game is in three days," Coach said. "Cooper will pitch. We'll be playing against the Groundhogs. They're tough, as you know."

The Groundhogs had defeated the Mustangs a couple of weeks before. The Mustangs won the other time they'd faced each other, so the teams were evenly matched.

Grandpa James was waiting for Rhino when he left the dugout. Rhino hugged him. He was already thinking about the playoffs, not the awards.

"We've got our momentum back," Rhino said. "We sure needed that win. And I need something else!"

"Let me guess—you're hungry," Grandpa said with a laugh.

"Hungry and thirsty," Rhino replied. "That was a long, hard game."

"What will it be?" Grandpa asked. "A hot dog from the refreshment stand or a PB&J at home?"

"I could eat both," Rhino said. A hot dog sounded delicious. "Let's start here."

Rhino squeezed some yellow mustard onto his hot dog and took a bite. Bella waved to Rhino and walked over to the picnic table.

"Is that the secret to your strength?" Bella asked, pointing to the hot dog. "Wish I could knock one over the fence like you do."

Rhino blushed. "I don't eat many hot dogs," he said. "Just on special occasions. I think my secret is Grandpa's cooking."

"I've got a secret, too," Bella said. "Something we're cooking up for the big awards dinner after the playoffs. I'll tell you about it Monday at school."

"What do I have to do?" Rhino asked.

"Oh, nothing hard. A little skit or something. You'll see."

"Just don't make me dance," Rhino said with a

grin. Bella and her friend Ariana performed as a dance team at the school talent show. "I dance about as well as you hit home runs. In other words, I don't."

"No dancing," Bella said. "Just some funny stuff. My dad is running the dinner, so he asked me to set something up for our team."

"Do we have to do the skit even if we don't win the championship?" Rhino asked.

"Sure. Why would that matter? A couple of the other teams will do a skit or something, too, so we want to be the best. I was going to ask Cooper and Carlos to be in it, too."

Rhino shrugged. "Count me in," he said.

"Okay, but don't tell anybody else. Remember, it's a surprise for the dinner. A secret."

Rhino ate the last bite of his hot dog, then wiped some mustard off his mouth with a napkin.

"I'm still hungry," he said to Grandpa. "Let's get home to that PB&J."

· CHAPTER 4 ·
Looking Back

Rhino usually ate lunch with a group of kids who loved to talk about dinosaurs or astronomy, like the stars or planets. But on Monday, Bella called a meeting with Cooper, Rhino, and Carlos to talk about their skit for the dinner.

"We need to do something funny," Bella said as they ate together in a corner of the cafeteria. "There will be lots of speeches about teamwork and sportsmanship. All of that is important, but I want to do something exciting! I want to make the guests laugh."

Rhino bit into his sandwich. He loved to laugh,

but baseball was serious business to him. Still, this wasn't all about baseball. The awards night was supposed to be relaxing and fun, not competitive.

"Here's my idea," Bella said. "Remember how excited we all were on the first day of practice? And how nervous?"

"I couldn't even eat my lunch that day," Carlos said, holding up his sandwich and staring at it like it was poison. "I'd hit a few plastic baseballs in the yard with my dad, but being on a team was a whole different thing. I was sure I'd swing and miss at every pitch."

"You were right," Rhino said as a joke, nudging Carlos with his elbow.

Carlos laughed. "I know. But by the end of the practice session I wasn't so nervous anymore. I wasn't the only one who couldn't hit the ball!"

"It shows you how much we've all improved, doesn't it?" Bella said. "That's a good message for the skit."

Rhino thought over the skills he'd learned that

spring. How to cover first base and wait for the right pitch instead of swinging hard at anything near the plate.

"Showing that we were scared is a good way to start," Cooper said. "Maybe we can do a skit with two batters. One is certain that he'll hit a home run every time, but then he doesn't hit a thing. The other is afraid that he'll keep striking out, but then he wallops the first pitch."

"I know who the overconfident one could be," Rhino said. "Dylan. Remember how he thought he was such hot stuff?"

"He was a bully, too," Carlos said. "Making fun of anybody who dropped the ball or struck out. We could do an entire skit about him."

Bella shook her head. "I know, but that wouldn't be nice at all," she said. "You have to admit that Dylan's been a much better teammate lately. Besides, he'll probably win at least one of the big awards. Let's not spoil his evening by making fun of him."

Rhino took a handful of BBQ chips and let out a sigh. Dylan had spoiled plenty of days for other people on the team. And if he scooped up most of the awards, where would that leave Rhino or his other teammates?

Dylan and Rhino weren't exactly friends, but they supported each other and worked together for the good of the team. *I deserve a big award as much as he does*, Rhino thought.

"So let's work on this," Bella said. "I like the idea of starting out nervous and making mistakes. Everybody can relate to that. By the end of the skit, we'll show how far we've come in just a couple of months. Beginners to champions!"

"We're not champions yet," Rhino said.

"But we will be, right?" Bella replied.

"I think so," Rhino said. "We've beaten every team at least once, so we should be able to do it again."

"I've heard that the pressure is triple in the

playoffs," Cooper said. "There's so much riding on every pitch. If you lose a game, your season's over."

Rhino didn't feel scared. He felt excited. "We've done well under pressure," he said. "The idea of performing this skit makes me more nervous than a game, though. The whole league will be watching. And listening!"

"So we'd better be good," Bella said. "We need to work on a script. How about meeting again on Wednesday at lunchtime? Bring some ideas."

"I like the ideas we already came up with," Rhino said.

"So do I," Bella replied. "But we still need a script. And practice. I don't want to mess this up. My dad's counting on us."

"Maybe we should scrap the skit and bring back the band," Cooper said. He'd played the drums in Mustang Rock. Rhino played guitar.

"Yeah," Carlos said. "I'm more confident singing than talking in front of a crowd."

"Not a bad idea," Bella said. "Maybe part of the skit can be a song. But it has to be about baseball. And being nervous."

Maybe it should be about the big awards, Rhino thought. That's what he was most nervous about. Baseball wasn't easy, but it was always fun. He didn't want to wait until next season to earn a big trophy like C.J.'s. He wanted one now.

Be patient, his thinker told him. *Helping my team win is much more important than a trophy.*

· CHAPTER 5 ·
A Crucial Injury

Most of the Mustangs' games had been on Saturdays, so a Tuesday evening playoff game was an exciting change. Parents and grandparents filled the bleachers, and many of the players from other teams lined the fence.

"There are way more people here than at any of our other games," Rhino said, tossing a ball to Carlos. Game time was still about ten minutes away.

Cooper was slowly warming up in the bullpen. The Groundhogs were out in left field, snagging fly balls and rolling grounders to one another. The

Groundhogs were the visiting team tonight, so they'd bat first.

Rhino couldn't wait to swing the bat for real. He'd scorched a few pitches in batting practice, sending them far over the fence.

"Bring it in!" Coach Ray called from the dugout.

Rhino caught one more throw from Carlos and ran in. "We need to be sharp today," Rhino said to Carlos. "And smart! Baseball is a thinking game, too."

Rhino put his thinker to work several times in the early innings. When a Groundhog player took a big lead off first base, Rhino caught Cooper's eye and gave him a signal that they'd talked about before, pulling on the brim of his cap. Cooper fired the ball to first base. Rhino made the catch and tagged the base runner as he slid.

The umpire swung his arm and jutted his thumb.

"Out!"

The Mustangs and their fans exploded in

cheers. It was their first pickoff of the season. Rhino didn't think any of the other teams had done one, either.

In the fourth inning, Rhino made another smart play. Dylan was on second base after smashing a double to lead off the inning. Everyone in the park was certain that Rhino would be swinging for the fences. But the game was still scoreless, so one run could be a huge advantage. Instead of trying for a power shot, Rhino tapped a beautiful bunt up the first-base line. He was thrown out, but Dylan made it to third. The Mustangs were on the verge of taking the lead.

Unfortunately, Carlos struck out and Gabe hit a lazy pop fly to end the inning.

"Should have swung away," Cooper mumbled, shaking his head as he and Rhino took the field.

"Next time," Rhino said. "Just keep pitching great."

Cooper continued his shutout pitching, but so did the Groundhogs' tall left-hander. For the first time all season, the Mustangs entered the sixth inning in a scoreless tie.

Rhino glanced up at the bleachers and saw Grandpa and C.J. They both waved. Rhino touched his cap and nodded slightly. *Big pressure now,* he thought. "Defense!" he yelled.

The leadoff hitter sent a sizzling ground ball up the middle for a single. He stayed close to the base while Cooper faced the next batter, remembering that his teammate had been picked off.

"Turn two!" Rhino called.

Cooper had yielded only two hits today, both singles. He'd pitched well, but a small letdown now could cost the Mustangs the game.

Cooper stayed solid. He struck out the next batter.

"Nice!" Rhino called. "Two more outs."

The Groundhogs' pitcher was up to bat now. As a lefty like Rhino, he was more likely to hit the ball toward the first-base side of the diamond, or into right field. Rhino bounced on his toes, ready to grab anything hit his way.

"Strike one!" called the umpire as Cooper blazed a fastball past the batter.

Rhino stepped over to first base, making sure the base runner wouldn't decide to take a bigger lead. Then he hustled back to the edge of the grass.

Crack! The ball made a quick bounce near the mound and streamed toward right field. It was deep in the hole between Rhino and Carlos, but Rhino had the better chance to stop it. He made a back-handed catch, and instantly sized up the situation. He was too far from first to beat the hitter, and Cooper was too late to cover. The smart play was to second base, where Dylan was running over from shortstop.

Rhino fired the ball to second, but Carlos was sprinting there, too. Dylan caught the ball and lunged for the sliding base runner. Carlos stumbled and let out a yelp.

The runners were safe at first and second base. The umpire called time-out and waved for Coach Ray to come onto the field. Carlos was lying on his back, holding his leg.

Rhino trotted over. "You got kicked?"

Carlos looked up and grimaced. "Right in the shin," he said. "Wow, that stings."

Coach handed Carlos a water bottle and carefully rolled down Carlos's sock. He pressed gently on the shin.

"I think it's okay," Carlos said.

Rhino helped Coach pull Carlos to his feet and take a few steps. "I'm fine," Carlos said, but his voice sounded as if he was in pain.

"We can't take a chance," Coach said. "Let's get you to the dugout."

Carlos frowned, but he walked to the dugout without help, limping a little. The spectators cheered, and all of the players clapped.

The Mustangs were in a jam. Runners on

first and second. One out. And a key infielder out of the game.

Coach looked around. A couple of other Mustangs had taken turns at second base early in the season, but Carlos had established himself as the best by far. Sara and Paul were in the dugout, and they'd played the first three innings. The league rules allowed for a player to return to the game to replace an injured teammate. Sara was awkward and not a great fielder, so Rhino was surprised when Coach called for her to come in.

Coach put his hand on Rhino's shoulder. "I need you to play second."

"Me?" Rhino had played first base for every inning of the season. Coach wanted him to switch? Now? In what might be the *last* inning for the Mustangs?

"Sara can play first base," Coach said. "We need a talented fielder at second. I know you can handle it."

Rhino looked at Cooper and Dylan.

"Do it for the Mustangs," Dylan said. "Coach is right. We need you."

Cooper gave Rhino a light punch on the arm. "It's just for two outs," he said. "You're the man."

Rhino swallowed hard. He turned to Sara and gave her a thumbs-up. Rhino had helped build Sara's confidence early in the season when she really needed it. Now Rhino was the one who needed a confidence boost.

Rhino inhaled deeply.

And he took his position near second base.

· CHAPTER 6 ·
Rising Pressure

This was like the beginning of the season all over again. Rhino felt nervous and unready at a position he'd never played.

At the most important moment of the season!

"One out!" Rhino called, trying to sound fearless. "Let's turn a double play!" But he was really hoping Cooper would strike out the next two batters.

Don't make a mistake, he told himself. *Don't give away a run. Or two!*

But then his thinker came through loud and clear. *Relax. You're a great player.*

"Any base!" Rhino yelled. With runners on first and second, the Mustangs could get a force-out on a grounder at first, second, or third.

Whack! The batted ball took a big hop. Dylan fielded it and turned toward second. Rhino was on his way, racing to get there before the base runner.

Rhino caught the ball and stepped on second base for an out. His momentum carried him toward third base, so it made sense to try for the double play there instead of twisting toward first.

Rhino leaped and threw as hard as he could. But his throw was way off course. The ball soared past the third baseman and rolled to the fence.

Rhino watched in agony as the runner rounded third and kept going. He slid into home before the third baseman reached the ball.

The batter ran easily to second base.

Rhino stared at the sky. He'd made a good play, and then a terrible throw. The scoreboard showed the damage. Groundhogs 1, Mustangs 0.

Three seconds, Rhino's thinker told him.

"Shake it off," Dylan said. "Let's get this next guy. We'll win the game in our next at bat."

Dylan would lead off again in the bottom of the sixth. If the Mustangs could get out of this inning just one run behind, they'd still have a strong chance to win.

Cooper threw a strike. And another.

Rhino let out his breath. Pounded his glove.

The batter hit the next pitch high in the air. The ball floated toward the outfield, but not very deep.

"I've got it!" Rhino called. He backpedaled a few steps and set up under the ball.

And made the catch for the third out.

Dylan raced over and clapped Rhino on the back. Cooper shook his hand. Sara gave him a thumbs-up.

"Great work out there," Coach said as Rhino picked up a bat. "Teamwork!"

Carlos held out his hand and Rhino slapped it. "How's the shin?" he asked.

"Sore," Carlos replied, pointing to the ice pack on his outstretched leg. "But I'll be fine for the next game. So let's make sure there *is* a next one!"

The Mustangs had managed only four hits today, and Dylan had two of them. He looked very confident as he stepped up to the plate, glaring at the pitcher and taking a few hard swings.

"Wait for your pitch," Rhino said from the on-deck circle.

Dylan didn't wait long. He lined the first pitch deep down the right-field line and reached second base standing up ahead of the throw.

"Knock him home!" Bella called.

Rhino felt a surge of energy. He could make up for that throwing error with one swing. One more of his trademark home runs would win this game for the Mustangs.

The first pitch looked good. A little low, a little outside, but very hittable. Rhino swung with all his might.

Swish! Rhino hit nothing as the ball zipped by.

Just make contact, his thinker said. *No more wild swings.*

He hit the next pitch, but it headed foul—over the bleachers behind the dugout.

Two strikes already. Rhino had to drive Dylan in. With Carlos out of the game, Sara was the next batter, and she'd only had a couple of hits all season.

Wham! Rhino connected with a solid swing and sent the ball flying into right-center field. He sprinted toward first base and heard the ball smash into the fence.

"Keep going!" called Coach. Rhino slid into second. Dylan crossed home with the tying run.

Back in business, Rhino thought. *Whole new ball game.*

The Groundhogs' coach called for time and walked to the mound. After giving up two straight doubles, the tall, left-handed pitcher was finished for the day. Rhino tried to relax while the new pitcher took some warm-up throws, but his mind was on one thing: *Score the winning run!*

Sara swung at the first pitch and missed. Then she watched one go by for a second strike.

Rhino wondered if he should run on the next pitch. Stealing third base was never easy, but maybe it was worth the risk. As the pitcher unleashed the ball, Rhino took off.

He heard a *plunk* and a big cheer from the crowd. The pitcher and catcher both scrambled toward the ball as it dribbled toward first base. Rhino steamed into third.

Sara was out, but Rhino stood just sixty feet from home! He was surprised that Sara had bunted with two strikes, since a fouled-off bunt counted as a third strike. But Sara had put the ball into fair territory.

"Come on, Gabe!" Rhino shouted to the next batter. The Mustangs' catcher was short but he had some power. If he hit the ball out of the infield, Rhino could score.

Rhino looked at his friends in the dugout. They'd all worked so hard this season. They

deserved to play in the championship game. Rhino could make sure that happened.

As soon as Gabe hit the ball, Rhino felt another energy burst. The ball flew into the outfield and the right fielder got under it. Rhino could run as soon as the ball was caught, as long as he stepped on third base first, so he kept his foot on the base and leaned toward home.

"Go!" shouted his teammates as the catch was made. Rhino sprinted hard, knowing that the throw was already on its way.

The ball bounced near the pitcher's mound, and the Groundhogs' catcher crouched in front of home plate. Rhino timed his slide perfectly. His foot hit the plate just before he was tagged. The umpire yelled that he was safe.

The Mustangs raced from the dugout and mobbed Rhino. They'd won!

"Don't forget Gabe," Rhino said. "He's the one who hit the ball!"

"And Sara, too," said Bella. "Her hit moved Rhino to third."

"Yeah, that was a gutsy move, Sara," Rhino said. "No one bunts with two strikes."

Sara blushed. "I didn't bunt. I swung as hard as I could, but I barely nicked the ball."

Rhino laughed. "It worked like a bunt. Got me to third base."

"Championship game, here we come!" Bella said.

· CHAPTER 7 ·
Error Terror?

Rhino packed his lunch most days, but pizza day was different. Grandpa gave him money to buy two slices. So, the day after the playoff win, Rhino joined Carlos, Bella, and Cooper for another meeting about the skit—this time with pizza.

Carlos was walking a little stiffly, but he insisted his shin was fine. "Just a tiny bruise," he said.

"Let's hear your ideas," Bella said.

None of the boys had any new ones. Rhino had put all his energy into baseball.

"The dinner is only two days away," Bella said. "Not much time."

But in between was the championship game on Thursday against the Sharks.

"Maybe we should just stick with what we came up with on Monday," Cooper said. "That way we can focus on the game."

"We came up with an *idea* on Monday," Bella said. "Not a script. We need to write one. And we need to practice."

"Are we going to play music?" Carlos asked. "I can bring my portable keyboard."

Bella shook her head. "I don't think you guys want to haul that equipment to the dinner. This is for fun. We can sing without instruments."

Rhino took out a pen and a notebook. "I'll write down the lyrics."

Everybody took a big bite of pizza and chewed slowly. No one had any idea what to say.

"Remember, it should be funny," Bella said.

Everybody took another bite.

"I guess it would be funny if we stood up there

and didn't sing at all," Carlos said. "Like we were too nervous to even speak."

"We don't want people laughing *at* us. We want them laughing *with* us," Bella said. "Remember, we started out nervous early in the season, but then we developed confidence."

"What rhymes with nervous?" Rhino asked.

"Nothing," Bella said. "But that's the right idea. Let's throw out some baseball words and find words that *do* rhyme. Then we can write a song around them."

"Error," Cooper said.

"Terror," said Rhino.

"Double," said Carlos.

"Trouble," Rhino replied.

Bella laughed. "See? You're good at this, Rhino. Let's try *homer.*"

"Roamer?" Rhino said. "Domer?"

"Is that even a word?" Cooper said. "Try *baseball.*"

No one had a good rhyme for that one.

"That's okay," Bella said. "We're making progress. Let's write some lines for that first pair. Error terror."

Rhino thought hard. Carlos cleared his throat and began speaking in a singsong voice. "I tried to catch a grounder, but made a stupid error, and every time I tried again, my brain froze up in terror."

Rhino nodded. "Not bad."

"Nice start, but making an error isn't stupid," Bella said. "Everybody makes them. So let's be more positive. Like, you make an error, but then you follow it up with some great catches. So you're getting rid of your terror, not building it up."

"Good point," Carlos said.

Rhino reached for his second slice of pizza. Bella pointed at him and said, "Write Carlos's line down first."

"I thought you didn't like it?"

"But it's worth keeping," Bella said. "We have to start with something, then make it better. So write it down and we'll keep writing new lines until we get it right."

Rhino wrote it down, but then he had a new idea. "What if the singer is saying that he expects to be a terror, but in a good way? Like a home-run terror—a batter who always swings for the fences? And he thinks he'll be a perfect fielder, too, and not make any errors. Hitting *terror*, never makes an *error*. Then the next line shows that he's not as good as he thinks he is."

"And he—or *she*—gets better after they put in some hard work," Bella said. "I like that. Always building up the positive but showing that it doesn't come easy."

Rhino looked at the clock. The lunch period had raced by. "That bell's going to ring in four minutes," he said, picking up his second slice of pizza. "Time to be an eating terror. I'm not wasting a single bite of this."

Bella put her palms on the table. "We can meet again tomorrow. We know what we need now, so

everybody think of some rhymes tonight. We'll wrap up the script tomorrow. Somehow we have to find a chance to practice, too."

"We made a lot of progress today," Rhino said. "At least now we know what we want to say."

Bella held up two fingers. "Two days," she said. "That's not much time. And we have a championship game tomorrow evening. Plus schoolwork."

"We'll be okay," Rhino said. "We've got four brains working on it. That ought to be enough."

· CHAPTER 8 ·
"Play Ball!"

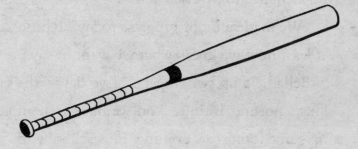

On Thursday, Rhino ate a light, early dinner with Grandpa and C.J. "I'll snack after the game," he said.

Rhino loved suiting up for the games, pulling his blue-and-white Mustangs jersey over his head, wiping any dust from his cleats, straightening his cap to look just right. Coach always said that looking sharp was an important part of the preparation. If you looked like a great player, you'd play like one.

Before they left for the field, Rhino took a few minutes to admire the trophies again. *My championship trophy can go right next to Grandpa's,* he thought.

And if I get a special award for best hitter or something, it can go behind my blue ribbon.

"Soon we'll need a bigger trophy shelf," Grandpa said from the doorway. "Ready to go?"

Rhino grabbed his glove and bat and hurried out the door.

At the field, he joined Cooper, Carlos, and Bella in right field. They formed a circle and tossed a ball back and forth, but they also tried out their song. They'd finally nailed down the lyrics during lunch that afternoon. Each of them took a turn singing a line. That way each one didn't have to memorize the whole song. Rhino already knew his lines by heart.

The energy and excitement seemed even higher tonight than for the first playoff game. "We're really here," Rhino said to Cooper as they sat in the dugout while the Sharks took infield practice. "We're playing for the championship!"

"Usual lineup and batting order," Coach said. "We bat first tonight. Dylan's pitching. Cooper can come in for an inning or two of relief if we need him."

Rhino took a sip of water. The evening was warm with a light breeze blowing in from center field. An announcer was reading the starting line-ups from a booth above the backstop. The smell of hot dogs and french fries filled the air.

The umpire yelled "Play ball!"

Rhino gripped his bat. "Let's get some base runners!" he called.

The Sharks were the hottest team in the league, having won their last four regular-season games before routing the Tigers in the playoffs. But the Mustangs had been the last team to beat them.

The Sharks' pitcher had a misleading curveball and a sinking fastball. He struck Cooper out on three pitches, and Bella only managed a slow grounder to the first baseman for the second out.

Rhino moved into the on-deck circle, but he was stranded there. Dylan hit a couple of foul balls before striking out.

"No problem," Rhino said. He trotted to first base and threw a series of hard grounders to the other infielders. He smiled as Carlos scooped one up and made a nice throw back.

"Good as new," Rhino said.

Carlos tipped his cap.

The Sharks' pitcher batted first, and he didn't waste any time. With a fierce swing, he sent Dylan's first pitch on a towering drive toward the fence. Bella drifted back and reached, but the ball was way over her head. Home run.

"Nice shot," Rhino mumbled as the pitcher ran past him.

"Okay, Dylan," he called. "Settle down. We'll get that run right back."

But the Sharks had several good hitters. Two singles and a long double gave them a 3–0 lead. The Mustangs were already looking up out of a deep hole as they headed for the dugout after one inning.

"Put us back in it, Rhino," Bella said.

"Blast one," added Cooper.

Rhino felt his heart beating fast. He took a deep breath. He'd faced this pitcher before and managed some hits, but he felt unusually nervous this time. The Sharks' big early lead didn't help.

He swung hard at the first pitch and missed. The Sharks cheered. Rhino stepped back and took another big breath. *One strike,* Rhino thought. *So what?* He felt better already. That was a good swing.

The second pitch was outside. Rhino stared at the pitcher until he caught his eye. The pitcher looked away. Rhino grinned.

Here came the curveball. Rhino timed his swing just right and connected. The ball zinged toward the scoreboard behind the center field fence. Rhino dropped his bat and sprinted.

But just before Rhino reached first base, the center fielder caught the ball. Rhino shook his head and trotted to the dugout.

"Beautiful shot," Coach said, bumping Rhino's fist with his own. "You threw a scare into them."

Carlos and Gabe both struck out. And the Sharks added another run in the bottom of the inning.

Now we're the ones who are scared, Rhino thought. *We need some runs!* But the Mustangs went down in order in the third inning, too. They hadn't produced a single base runner all game.

"Not a great way to end the season," Cooper said. "We need a spark."

"Next inning," Rhino said. "Top of the order."

But Dylan was shaky in the bottom of the third. He walked two batters. When a Shark smashed one off the fence in left field for a double, the Mustangs were six runs behind.

Coach called time-out and walked to the mound. Gabe trotted up from behind the plate, and Rhino ran over, too.

"Tired arm?" Coach asked.

Dylan shook his head. "My arm's fine. They're just pounding my pitches today."

"It's too early to bring in Cooper," Coach said. "Think you can settle down?"

Dylan frowned and gave a quick nod. He looked angry.

"We do it for the Mustangs, remember?" Rhino said.

Dylan nodded. Then he struck out two batters to end the inning. That fired up his teammates. They ran to the dugout ready to score some runs.

Cooper drew a walk. Bella bunted him to second.

Rhino waited with Dylan in the on-deck circle. "Get on base and I'll cut that lead in half," Rhino said.

"I'm clearing the bases," Dylan said. "First good pitch is going over the fence."

"Just connect," Rhino said. "One run at a time."

Dylan hit the first pitch over the shortstop's head, and Cooper raced home with the Mustangs' first run of the game.

Rhino took a couple of swings and stepped into the batter's box. He was thinking *home run*. But any solid base hit would be fine. Swinging for the fences often meant striking out.

Be smart here, he told himself. *One run is better than none.*

· CHAPTER 9 ·
Six Runs Down

The Sharks' pitcher certainly remembered Rhino's deep fly ball in the second inning. Another couple of feet and it would have been a home run. So he pitched cautiously, keeping the ball low and inside. The first two pitches were balls.

Come on, Rhino thought. *Pitch to me.*

The third pitch was even closer. Rhino leaned back and didn't flinch.

"Ball three," said the umpire.

Usually, a batter will not swing at a pitch if the count is three balls and no strikes. The odds are that there'll be another ball, and taking a walk is a safe strategy.

Rhino looked over at Coach Ray, who gave him the sign to swing if the pitch was good.

But the pitch was high and outside. Rhino rolled his bat to the dugout and ran to first base.

"Come on, Carlos!" Rhino yelled. The batters after Carlos were not strong hitters, so it was crucial for Dylan and Rhino to do some smart base running. Again, Rhino looked to Coach for a sign. Coach indicated a double steal. Rhino made sure Dylan saw the sign, too.

The pitcher tossed the ball to the first baseman, and Rhino hustled back before the tag. *They know something's up,* Rhino thought. *But we're stealing. On this pitch.*

The pitcher threw, and Rhino and Dylan took off. But the catcher had wisely called for a pitch-out. He caught the ball and hurled it to third. Dylan slid under the third baseman's glove, but it looked like he was out.

Instead, the ball rolled free. Dylan was safe. So was Rhino.

The Mustangs in the dugout went wild.

Make contact, Carlos, Rhino thought as he stood on second base. *Get us home.*

Carlos hit the ball sharply to the second baseman, who looked home but then threw to first. Dylan scored and Rhino raced to third.

Two outs. The Mustangs had trimmed the lead to 6–2.

Gabe struck out to end the inning with Rhino still at third.

No easy runs in this game, Rhino thought. But at least they were on the scoreboard.

Dylan pitched a 1-2-3 inning in the fourth, looking much steadier than in the early innings. Rhino cheered for every Mustang batter in the fifth, but it looked like the sixth would be their next opportunity to score. He was surprised when Sara lined a two-out single into left field.

Cooper followed with a run-scoring double.

They'd pulled closer, but not close enough. Dylan pitched another strong inning. The Mustangs entered the sixth (and final) inning down 6–3.

"It's up to us again," Rhino said to Dylan, who put on a batting helmet to lead off.

"Who better than us?" Dylan replied.

"We've done it all season," Rhino said. "Let's go!"

Rhino felt his heart beating hard as Dylan and the Sharks' pitcher began a lengthy battle. Ball one. Strike one. Ball two. Strike two. A couple of long foul balls. Another ball.

And a high, outside fastball for ball four.

Time for a big swing. But even a home run wouldn't tie the score. The Mustangs batting after Rhino would have a lot of work to do, too.

Pitch to me this time, Rhino thought. *No more safe throws.* He glared at the pitcher and waited until the pitcher met his eyes. Rhino nodded slightly. *Bring it on!*

Wham. Rhino's powerful swing sent the ball deep into the gap between the left fielder and center.

He was nearly to second base before the center fielder picked up the ball, and he continued at full speed as he headed for third.

Dive, he told himself as the ball bounced a few feet from the third baseman. Rhino stretched his arms in a cloud of dirt and reached the base just in time. A triple! And an important RBI.

Rhino popped up and brushed the dirt from the front of his jersey. He tasted sweat dripping down his face.

Rhino gave three steady claps and yelled to Carlos. "Bring me home! Let's do it!"

Carlos hadn't had a hit in either playoff game. Rhino stayed alert, ready to scoot for home if the pitcher threw a wild pitch.

But Carlos banged the ball up the middle, and Rhino scored easily. They'd trimmed the lead to one run, 6 5.

Gabe followed with a double. The Mustangs had runners on second and third with no outs.

That was enough for the Sharks' coach. He pointed to the shortstop and had him switch positions with the pitcher.

"We can do this!" Rhino said. "We can be champions."

Carlos and Gabe stayed stuck on the bases as the next two Mustangs struck out.

Rhino shut his eyes. The Mustangs were still a run behind and down to their final batter.

"Another big hit, Sara," Rhino called. Sara had never had two hits in a game. That single an inning before was the first base hit she'd had in a month.

But Sara shocked everybody with a line drive up the middle. Carlos scored the tying run. Gabe rounded third but hurried back when the pitcher caught the throw from the outfield.

Cooper grounded out, but the Mustangs were still alive. A 6–6 tie going to the bottom of the sixth.

"Defense!" shouted Rhino as he grabbed his glove. The Mustangs had mounted an incredible comeback, but just one run would win it for the Sharks.

And it didn't take long before it looked like that would happen. Dylan gave up a single, Carlos bobbled a ground ball for an error, and Dylan issued a walk to load the bases with one out.

Coach Ray called time-out.

"You gave it all you've got, Dylan," Coach said as Rhino, Cooper, and Gabe joined him on the mound. He handed the ball to Cooper.

All of the Mustangs clapped and yelled as Dylan walked to shortstop. So did the spectators. Dylan looked at the ground, but finally he touched the brim of his cap to say thanks.

Rhino stared at the scoreboard while Cooper warmed up. He didn't need to look. He knew the situation. 6–6. Bottom of the sixth. If the Sharks scored, it was over.

But Cooper came through. Six pitches. Two strikeouts.

Extra innings to decide the title!

And Rhino would be batting third.

Bella stroked a hard shot to third base, and just missed beating the throw to first for the first out.

Dylan was angry again. He'd nearly lost the game with some wild pitching. He watched an outside pitch go past, then walloped the ball deep into right field.

The crowd gasped.

But the ball fell short and the outfielder made the catch.

Just like that, the Mustangs had two outs.

Everything rested on Rhino's shoulders. All eyes were on him.

He felt strangely calm. He'd been in this position before. Game on the line.

The pitch was fast, but the ball looked like a giant beach ball to Rhino. He unleashed a steady, powerful swing.

The outfielders never moved. They just turned and watched the ball soar far over their heads.

Home run. The farthest one he'd ever hit.

The Mustangs had stormed all the way back from a 6–0 hole and taken the lead. Rhino raced around the bases and stomped hard on home plate.

Cooper took it from there, sending the Sharks down to defeat with three quick outs.

"We did it!" Rhino shouted, racing to the mound and celebrating with his teammates. "We did it! We did it! We did it!"

The Mustangs were the champions.

· CHAPTER 10 ·
Many Valuable Players

The night of the awards dinner, Rhino sat at a big, round table with his teammates. All of the other teams had tables of their own. Grandpa James, C.J., and lots of other people were in attendance, too.

All of the players were wearing their team caps, but they weren't dressed for a game. Rhino looked sharp in a white shirt and blue tie—Mustangs colors. His teammates were dressed up, too.

They enjoyed a dinner of chicken, ziti, and vegetables, then the coaches gave out trophies to everyone except the Mustangs. They'd get their championship trophies a little later in the evening.

Coach Ray was in charge of the announcements, and he reminded the players of the most important things about sports: to work hard, be patient, and always have fun. A few members of the Groundhogs stood up and sang "Take Me Out to the Ball Game."

"Our turn," Bella said, waving for Rhino, Cooper, and Carlos to join her at the front of the room.

"This has been a great season, and we want to thank all of the coaches, umpires, players, and everyone who took part," Bella said. "We thought it would be fun to remember what it was like just a few months ago, back before we knew what we were doing. A lot of us thought we'd step right in and be baseball heroes. It wasn't so easy. If it wasn't for our coaches and our teammates' support, we'd probably still be trying to figure out how to catch the ball!"

Bella started singing, "It's the first day of practice, and I can't wait!"

"I'll hit the ball a mile, and slide into the plate," sang Carlos.

Rhino chimed in. "I'll smack a couple homers, and be a fielding terror."

"I'll pitch a dozen strikeouts, and never make an error," Cooper finished.

Bella crouched low, making believe she was an umpire. Rhino kneeled in front of her like a catcher. Cooper faced them from a few yards away, and Bella called, "Batter up!"

Carlos gave the audience a big smile and stepped up with an imaginary bat. He pointed to a spot high and far away and said, "Watch this," with all the confidence he could muster.

Cooper pretended to pitch. Carlos swung.

"Strike one!" yelled Bella.

Cooper quickly went through the motions of another pitch, and Carlos swung so hard he spun completely around.

"Strike two!" said Bella.

Carlos fell down after his third wild swing.

"You're out," Bella called. "Next batter!"

Carlos and Rhino switched spots. As Rhino

swung at Cooper's pitch, Bella made a loud *thwack* sound with her mouth.

"A high pop-up!" Carlos announced. "Get under it, Cooper."

Cooper circled around, waiting a *long* time for the imaginary ball to come down. "I've got it," he said. "It's all mine."

Cooper stuck out a hand, then pretended to bobble the ball. He groaned as it fell through his fingers, then made believe he was chasing it along the ground.

"A costly error," Bella said. "I don't think these guys will *ever* get it." She turned to the audience. "Do you?"

Everyone cheered. Rhino, Cooper, and Carlos bowed.

Cooper began the rhyme this time. "We started slow and learned a lot."

"We started cold and ended *hot*," said Carlos, fanning himself with his cap.

Bella picked up the next line. "We started worried and ended bold."

"We started young and ended . . ." Rhino sang, and the other three joined him for the closing word: "Champions!"

Rhino lifted his arms and smiled at the crowd. There were so many great things about baseball. Having teammates was the best. They had become his closest friends.

Coach Ray stepped up to the microphone again. He called all of the Mustangs to come up, and he handed each one a championship trophy.

Rhino stared at the engraving on the trophy as he took his seat.

MUSTANGS
LEAGUE CHAMPIONS

Each coach gave out special awards to a few players on their teams. When it was Coach Ray's turn, he said he'd had to make some tough decisions.

"We relied on two pitchers for most of the season, and they both were outstanding," Coach said.

"But Cooper was the winning pitcher in both play-off games, so he gets our award for Best Pitcher."

Rhino yelled and clapped Cooper on the back. Then he glanced at Dylan, who was clapping but looked a little glum.

Dylan brightened right away. Coach called him up for the Best Hitter award. Rhino had been hoping that he'd win it instead.

"We had a lot of talented fielders, too," Coach said. "But guess who made the fewest errors? My own daughter, Bella. She gets the Best Fielder award."

Rhino smiled at Bella, but inside he felt a little sad. There was only one award left. Most Improved. Coach was already pointing to Carlos and asking him to come up.

Rhino stood and cheered for all of his teammates. Carlos really deserved the trophy for most improved player. Rhino shook his hand when Carlos returned. He looked around at the four special trophies on the table. *They all deserve them,* his thinker told him. Being on a team with these players had been more rewarding than he ever could have imagined. Rhino hadn't won any of the major awards, but he was fine with that. There were many more baseball seasons ahead of him.

He turned and saw Grandpa and C.J. sitting at a table with Cooper's parents. Rhino gave them a thumbs-up.

"Before we go, there's one more trophy," Coach announced. "This isn't just a Mustangs award. It's for the whole league. The other coaches all agreed on this one, and they decided that I should present it. It covers the best things about sports. Leadership. Sportsmanship. Teamwork. And, yes, baseball skills. Great fielding and hitting and baserunning. The things that make someone more than a player. A *most valuable* player."

Rhino's eyes grew wide. Bella, Cooper, Carlos, and the others were all looking at him. "This is the *real* secret," Bella whispered.

Rhino took a deep breath.

Coach held up a tall trophy. "This year's most valuable player is from my team, the Mustangs," he said. "Come on up here, Ryan Howard. This trophy is for you!"

LET THE GAME BEGIN!

SEE WHERE IT ALL STARTED
LITTLE RHINO #1!

YOU CAN'T HIT WITHOUT A BAT!

BATTER UP WITH
LITTLE RHINO #2!

LET THEM SEE YOUR TALENT!

CHECK OUT
LITTLE RHINO #4!